O9-BUB-446

DUNGEON CRAWL!

Published in the United States by Random House Children's Books, a division of Penguin Random House LLC, 1745 Broadway, New York, NY 10019, and in Canada by Penguin Random House Canada Limited, Toronto. Random House and the colophon are registered trademarks of Penguin Random House LLC.

rhcbooks.com
minecraft.net

Library of Congress Cataloging-in-Publication Data is available upon request.

ISBN 978-1-9848-5065-2 (trade)—ISBN 978-1-9848-5066-9 (lib. bdg.)—
ISBN 978-1-9848-5067-6 (ebook)

Cover design by Diane Choi

Printed in the United States of America

10 9 8 7 6 5 4 3 2 1

MOJANG

MINECRAFT

WOODSWORD CHRONICLES

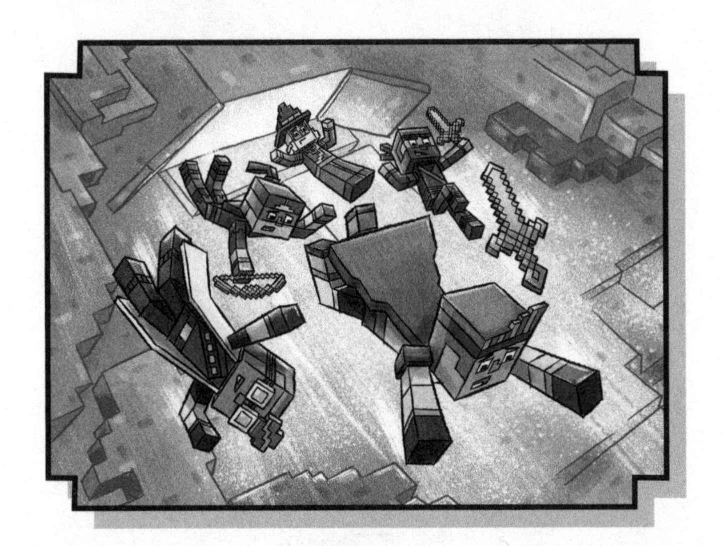

DUNGEON CRAWL!

By Nick Eliopulos
Cover illustrated by Luke Flowers
Interior illustrated by Chris Hill

Random House New York

MORGAN

ASH

HARPER

PLAYERS!

DOC CULPEPPER

IT'S ONLY FAIR TO TELL YOU NOW: THE EVOKER KING WINS IN THE END. . . .

Five unlikely heroes stood shoulder to shoulder in the dark. They had traveled great distances and overcome many threats. **Now they were deep underground**—deeper than they'd ever been. And they needed to go deeper still.

The fate of the world depended on the success of their quest.

The alchemist held out a potion. "Does anyone need healing?" she asked.

The knight hefted his shield. "Not me. Between my shield and this diamond armor, nothing's been able to touch me."

The rogue twirled her sword. **"I'D TAKE**

ANOTHER INVISIBILITY POTION," she said. "It makes my sneak attack unbeatable."

The wizard stroked his beard. "I'm glad you're on our side, you rascal," he said, chuckling.

The ranger strung her bow. "If everyone is ready, we should push forward," she said.

They were heroes. They were a team. And they were confident that they could handle anything this dungeon threw at them.

If only they knew what awaited them.

If only they knew they had played right into their enemy's hands.

If only they knew that this time . . . **they would lose.**

Chapter 1

"STEP INTO MY PARLOR!" IT'S THE POLITE WAY TO SAY: "COME HERE, I'M GONNA EAT YOU NOW."

The nights weren't as scary as they used to be.

Po Chen looked up at the full moon. It wasn't like the moon back home. **This moon was square and pixelated.** *Blocky.*

Recently, Po and his friends had discovered that their science teacher's virtual-reality headsets were special . . . really special. **The headsets transported them here, to a world that looked and behaved almost exactly like Minecraft.** As far as Po could tell, he and his friends were somehow *inside* the game. It was exhilarating and mysterious . . . **and scary.**

Because Po and his friends weren't alone. This

world was full of creatures—**or mobs,** as they were called in Minecraft. Not all of them were friendly. And many of the most dangerous mobs came out at night.

Po and his friends used to hide as soon as the sun went down. But that was before they'd found the materials to craft powerful weapons and armor. And more important, that was before **they'd learned to work as a team.**

Now, on this night, Po and his friends weren't hiding. **They were hunting.**

"I HOPE WE SEE A SPIDER SOON," he whispered. "And that's something I never imagined I'd say out loud."

"We'll find one eventually," Ash Kapoor said. Po still thought of her as the new girl at school, but she'd been with them for nearly all of their Minecraft adventures. **"SPIDERS ARE FAIRLY COMMON IN FORESTS LIKE THIS ONE."**

"And if we don't have any luck here, we can start checking caves," said Morgan Mercado. He was one of Po's oldest friends. **"IT MIGHT BE EASIER TO FIND SPIDERS IN A CAVE, ACTUALLY. THEIR BEADY LITTLE EYES GLOW RED IN THE DARK."**

Morgan and Ash were like walking encyclopedias for Minecraft. That was helpful . . . except on the rare occasions when this place didn't follow the rules.

"This is so typical," Jodi Mercado complained. She was Morgan's little sister, and she loved *most* animals—just not the creepy-crawly ones. **"THE ONE TIME WE WANT TO SEE A SPIDER, THERE AREN'T ANY AROUND!"**

"We could split up," suggested Harper Houston. "Then we could cover a larger area."

Harper was one of the smartest people Po had ever met. But that didn't sound like a particularly smart plan to him.

"Absolutely not," he said. **"DON'T SPLIT THE PARTY!"**

"Don't what the what?" asked Jodi.

"Don't split the party," Po repeated. "In other words: We need to stick together. It's the first rule of surviving a cooperative game!"

Harper rolled her square eyes. "I'm sorry. Are we *really* supposed to take strategic advice from a guy dressed like an insect?"

Po looked down at his digital avatar skin. He was pretty sure his *real* body was back in the school computer lab.

When they were in this game world, Morgan looked like Morgan, and Ash looked like Ash. **Their avatars were just blocky versions of themselves.** But they didn't have to be.

Po liked changing up his look. He put a lot of thought into his appearance, choosing a different skin almost every time he slipped on his headset. Today, he'd chosen to look like a humanoid housefly. His body was black and shiny. He had a pair of cute little wings attached to his back, but they were just for show.

"I FIGURED SOMEBODY NEEDED TO BE THE BAIT FOR THIS SPIDER HUNT," he said, puffing out his chest heroically. "But if you want me to shoo . . ."

"You'll do, Po-fly," said Jodi, and she patted Po's wings affectionately.

Ash was walking at the front of the group, and **Po noticed immediately when she stopped moving.** She waved her blocky fist to get their attention.

"Over there," she whispered, and she pointed through the trees. **Po saw a pair of beady eyes** in the shadows beneath the forest canopy. They glowed red in the dark.

"Let's get a little closer," Ash said. "Quietly!

Then when we're close, we can surprise it."

They crept forward. Po didn't even bother taking his sword out yet. A single spider wasn't much of a threat.

He moved forward slowly. Slowly . . .

Way too slowly.

"Hey, what gives?" he said. He felt stuck to the ground. Moving forward took far more effort than it should.

"COBWEBS," said Ash.

Ash was right. In the dark forest, Po had missed them completely. They'd all waded hip-deep into a thick net of webbing.

"Webs in a forest?" Morgan said. "And this many of them? Something isn't right."

"IT'S THE EVOKER KING," said Jodi. "He's messed with us before. And he's doing it again."

At the sound of their enemy's name, Po felt a chill. For as long as they'd been coming to this place, they'd seen evidence of a being who called himself the Evoker King.

They had learned long ago that the

Evoker King was able to bend the rules of Minecraft.

And if that wasn't scary enough, they had recently learned something new: the Evoker King wasn't a person at all, but an Artificial Intelligence set loose in the game.

Po shivered at the thought of what an AI could accomplish in a world built out of computer code. **Unfortunately, Po's involuntary shiver sent a vibration through the cobwebs . . .** and right to the spider.

The red eyes up ahead turned to look at him.

So did another set of eyes to the left.

And a third set to the right.

There were red eyes all around them, even *above* them, looking down from the trees. They twinkled like bloodred stars.

Po suddenly regretted his choice of outfit. **He didn't like the idea of being a fly caught in a web.**

And he decided that maybe the nights here were still a bit scary after all.

The hunters were now the hunted.

Chapter 2

DON'T BLAME THE SCARECROW FOR BEING CREEPY. IT'S SORT OF HIS WHOLE JOB.

Jodi tugged at the cobwebs surrounding her. She wasn't completely stuck, but the webs were slowing her down. **And the oncoming spiders clearly didn't have the same problem.** They skittered over the sea of webbing at full speed.

"Somebody do something!" buzzed Po. "I must look delicious right now!"

"THERE'S NO TIME TO ESCAPE," Ash said. "We have to fight."

Morgan held up his sword. "They're coming right to us, so just be ready to hit them when they get close!" he said. "If you time your swing right, you'll be okay."

"Don't miss, don't miss," Jodi muttered under her breath. She held her sword like a baseball bat. She waited as a spider came closer . . . closer . . .

SHE SWUNG! The sword knocked the spider backward. It recovered quickly, and it pounced once more, but Jodi was ready. A second hit was enough to destroy it. **The spider flopped onto its back and disappeared in a puff of pixels.**

"I should play more baseball," Jodi said.

"Don't let your guard down," Harper said. "There are more spiders where that came from."

"WE WANTED SPIDERS," said Jodi, readying her sword again. **"WE GOT SPIDERS."**

"Be careful what you wish for," said Po as the next one moved in for the attack.

When the last spider fell, Jodi and the others turned their attention to the cobwebs. Using their swords, they hacked a path through the sticky strands until they were all free. Ash picked up the strings left behind, and **Harper went around to collect the loot that had been dropped by the spiders.**

"Beautiful!" said Harper. "I was hoping for a spider eye or two. But there are at least ten here."

"SO DO YOU HAVE EVERYTHING YOU NEED FOR YOUR POTIONS?" Jodi asked.

"More than I need," said Harper. "Between these eyes and the blaze powder that the Librarian left for us, we're in good shape. Let's head back."

"I remember the way," Ash said. Jodi was always impressed with Ash's sense of direction. **It was**

just one of many talents Ash had honed as a Wildling Scout.

Ash led them out of the woods, over a hill, and toward a small blocky structure in the distance.

"HOME, SWEET HOME," said Morgan.

"It's not much of a home," said Jodi, and she made a face. The bunker was just so *basic:* a plain gray cube with a single door and no windows. She had wanted to make it a pyramid, or an obelisk— or a llama-shaped tower! But the group had asked her not to spend time or materials on a temporary shelter. **It was simply a place to store their beds and crafting materials while they got ready for their next big mission.**

"SPAWN POINT, SWEET SPAWN POINT," she said with a sigh.

There was one artistic addition that Jodi had insisted on, though. She saw it now as they got closer. A blocky human-shaped figure stood watch over their shelter. He had a body of hay, wooden-fence limbs, and a carved pumpkin for a head.

Jodi had named their new friend **Scarecrow Joe.**

"Hi, Joe!" said Po, and he waved at the scarecrow. "What's new?"

The scarecrow, of course, said nothing.

"I don't think he likes me very much," Po stage-whispered to Jodi. **She giggled.**

Harper got right to work. She walked up to the cauldron that they'd left just outside the shelter. "The spider eyes were the last ingredient I needed. **NOW I CAN FINALLY MAKE THESE POTIONS."**

"And then we'll be ready?" asked Morgan.

"I don't know if we'll *ever* be ready to face the

Evoker King." Harper shrugged. "But after this, we'll have everything on your list."

Morgan hopped up and down with excitement. **He had drawn up a wish list of items: potions, arrows, diamond armor, and enchanted swords.** They were all things that he thought would help them in their mission.

Ash put a hand on Harper's shoulder. "We can do this, Harper. Remember what the Librarian said? She told us that we'd find the source of the Evoker King's power at the heart of the world. Coordinates zero, zero." Ash pointed at their map. "We're close. And we've been preparing for days. If we're not ready now, we never will be."

"YOU'RE NOT READY," said a voice.

Jodi looked around. Was it her imagination, or had that voice come from . . . ?

"Over here," said the scarecrow.

"Scarecrow Joe . . . ?" she said.

"Not Joe," said Morgan. He drew his sword. "I recognize that voice. **IT'S THE EVOKER KING!"**

The scarecrow's eyes lit up. It turned its head to look at them and chuckled.

"That's impossible," Ash muttered. But Jodi knew that the "impossible" was often possible in Minecraft, if you got creative enough. **And while the Evoker King wasn't exactly a creative type, he seemed to be really good at breaking the rules.**

"Put your weapons away," said the Evoker King. **"I'M NOT HERE TO FIGHT YOU. I'M HERE TO HELP."**

"Yeah, right," said Po. He didn't put his sword away, and neither did anyone else.

"The path forward is full of danger," said

the King. **"THE ITEM YOU SEEK IS DEEP BENEATH THE GROUND, LOCKED AWAY WITHIN A DUNGEON.** You have no hope of reaching it. The dungeon is more than you can handle."

"You have no idea what we can handle," said Ash. **"WE'RE NOT AFRAID OF YOUR DUNGEON."**

"And we're not afraid of you," said Morgan.

"This is your final warning," said the King. **"TURN BACK NOW. TURN BACK . . . BEFORE IT'S TOO LATE."**

And with that, the scarecrow burst into flame!

Jodi flinched from the fire. "Joe!" she cried.

"THAT GUY IS THE WORST," Po said.

"He's not really a guy," said Harper.

"HE WAS TRYING TO SCARE US," said Ash.

"And that means *he's* scared," said Morgan. "He knows we're close to defeating him!"

Jodi squinted into the flames. "Do you hear that, Evoker King?" She shook her blocky fist in defiance. **"WE'RE COMING FOR YOU, YOU CREEP!"**

Chapter 3

ALL THE WORLD'S A STAGE. AND ALL OF US, MERELY PEOPLE IN CHICKEN OUTFITS.

Woodsword Middle School was practically vibrating with excitement. Students clustered in tight groups, bouncing in place before the morning bell. The chatter in the hallway was louder than ever.

Po felt the excitement in his bones. **He tapped his fingers on the spinning wheels of his wheelchair.** "This might be the best day of school ever," he said.

"Oh, I don't know," Morgan said. "The field trip to the landfill was pretty great."

"*Nobody* liked that field trip," Po said. He turned in his chair and gave Morgan a suspicious look. "What's wrong, buddy? You look sort of . . . **green.**"

It was true. Morgan looked queasy. There were bags under his eyes, too, as if he hadn't slept.

Morgan sighed. **"I'm nervous,"** he said. "I've never tried out for a play before."

"None of us have," said Po. **"That's what makes it so exciting!"**

Po had been quietly waiting for this day for a long time. Years, in fact. Every winter, the older students at Woodsword put on a play. **Everyone participated—some as actors, some as dancers or singers, and some on the backstage tech crew.**

When he was a younger kid, Po had marveled at the performances. He could still remember the Russian dances of *The Nutcracker,* the cardboard-sword duels of *Romeo and Juliet,* and the papier-mâché chains rattled by the ghosts of *A Christmas Carol.*

This year, Po and his friends were "the older students." It was finally their turn to put on a show.

Po hoped to be front and center.

"Don't be nervous, pal," Po said to Morgan. "If you don't want to be onstage, you can just sign up for the tech crew."

Morgan frowned. "Here's the thing, though—I *want* an acting part. Even though I'm super nervous about it." He shrugged. "Is that weird?"

"Not at all." Po patted his friend's arm. **"I love playing basketball, and I always have. But I still get nervous before every single game."**

"Really?" Morgan asked.

"Really," Po answered.

They'd arrived at the auditorium, where their whole grade was gathering. **Classes had been canceled for the morning** so that Ms. Minerva could get through all the tryouts before lunch. Students were supposed to study while they waited for their turn to audition.

Po and Morgan got in the line at the side of the stage. **They could see Harper and Jodi sitting together, going through a stack of flash cards.**

"There's a simple trick I use whenever I start to feel nervous," Po told Morgan. "I close my eyes for a few seconds, and I focus on breathing. In and out. In and out. And I tell myself that no matter what happens, I'll be okay."

"And that really works?" Morgan asked.

"Most of the time," said Po. **"Sometimes I'm forced to rely on plan B, which is to imagine that everybody but me is dressed like a chicken."** He rubbed his chin. "But that is *risky,* because you don't want to start laughing when you're trying to line up a three-point shot."

Morgan chuckled. Some of the color had come back to his face. "Thanks, Po," he said. "I'll keep that in mind." He peered over the heads of the students in front of them. **"I just hope this line moves before I completely lose my nerve!"**

Po watched from the wings while Morgan took the stage. His friend shook with nervous energy in the spotlight. But Po saw the moment Morgan closed his eyes and took a deep breath. When he opened his eyes again, his trembling had stopped.

"Hello, Morgan," said Ms. Minerva. She was seated in the front row of the auditorium. Beside her was **Ash, who had volunteered to be the stage manager.** As far as Po could tell, the stage manager did a little bit of everything.

"Are you trying out for an acting role?" Ash

asked, glancing at her clipboard. "Or singing?"

"Acting!" Morgan blushed a deep shade of pink. "Definitely acting."

Po chuckled. **The last time Morgan had sung the national anthem, Baron Sweetcheeks, the class hamster, had buried himself in wood chips to escape the noise.**

But Po had to hand it to Morgan: he was a good actor. Morgan's tryout went well, and by the time it was over, his nervousness was forgotten. He beamed a smile at Po and gave a thumbs-up when he walked off stage. "You're up, buddy!" he said.

Po wheeled himself to the center of the stage. **The spotlight was brighter than he'd expected.** He had to shield his eyes to see Ms. Minerva and Ash, even though they were directly in front of him.

They looked surprised to see him.

"Po?" said Ash. "Don't you have basketball this season?"

"Well, yeah." Po grinned. **"It wouldn't be much of a season without the MVP."**

"Is that going to be a problem?" Ash asked. Po squinted and saw that she was asking their teacher.

Ms. Minerva cleared her throat. **"An acting role is a big commitment, Po,"** she said. "It takes time to memorize lines. And missing a single rehearsal can throw off the entire production."

Po hadn't thought about that. He'd assumed he'd be able to do *both* things. Could he take some time away from basketball? And just thinking about what his coach would say about that made his stomach flip.

"What about tech crew?" Ash suggested. "We could give you a pretty important job backstage. **We could put you in charge of all the lights!"** She looked from Ms. Minerva to Po and back again. "It's a big job. But if you miss a few rehearsals, it won't matter so much."

Ms. Minerva nodded. **"I think that's a great solution, Ash.** What do you think, Po?"

Po's mouth went dry. He didn't know what to do. He didn't want to *run* the spotlights. He wanted to be *in* one.

At first, Po didn't say anything. He didn't want was to seem ungrateful, or to cause problems for his friends. And he hadn't thought about his

basketball schedule.

"That sounds great," he said**. He put on a happy face. "Thanks, Ash."**

Ms. Minerva smiled and turned her attention to the next student while Ash grinned at him and wrote something on her clipboard.

Look at me, Po thought. *I nailed my acting audition and nobody even knows it.*

Chapter 4

YOU CAN'T GO HOME AGAIN! (WELL, YOU CAN, BUT YOU MIGHT NOT LIKE WHAT YOU FIND THERE.)

When they first came to the field, **Harper thought it was a graveyard.**

Play auditions were over, and school was out for the day, so Harper and her friends had returned to Minecraft. **They'd left their temporary shelter for good, and they had continued their march toward coordinates 0,0 of the very center of this world.**

They were nearly there when they came across the field. It was a vast expanse of green. Every few yards, a piece of granite stood atop the grass. The blocks looked to Harper almost like simple tombstones. But they were something else entirely.

"MY SCULPTURES!" said Jodi. "What happened to them?"

Harper gasped. Jodi was right. She and her friends had been here before. . . .

This was the site of Jodi's sculpture garden. She'd spent hours on it during their earliest visits, before they'd even heard the name Evoker King. They'd left the sculptures behind many weeks ago. But this world had no wind, no decay, no *erosion.* **Harper had expected those sculptures to stand forever.**

"What *happened*?" Jodi said again. "These were my masterpieces! They've all been reduced to rubble."

"Our castle doesn't look much better," Morgan

said. He stood atop a nearby hill. **"COME SEE FOR YOURSELVES."**

Harper and the others climbed the hill to stand beside Morgan. From there, they had a view of the castle they'd built together, back when Ash had first joined them. Or rather, they had a view of what was left of the castle.

It had been picked apart. **All the doors and decorations were gone.** Random blocks were missing from the walls and turrets.

"Our castle," Harper said sadly. **"IT LOOKS LIKE . . . OLD, HAUNTED RUINS."**

"It looks more like Swiss cheese!" Jodi said. "This is the Evoker King's doing, isn't it?"

"Maybe," Ash said. "Or maybe the Librarian really needed the materials? It would be hard to be mad, in that case. We haven't seen her recently, but she's left a lot of materials behind to help us."

"ANYWAY, STUFF YOU MAKE IN MINECRAFT ISN'T SUPPOSED TO BE PERMANENT," Morgan said. He patted his sister on her on the edge of one of her square shoulders. **"IT ALL GETS RECYCLED EVENTUALLY."**

"Speaking of recycling, I can't believe we're all the way back to where we started!" said Po. "We basically traveled in a huge circle."

"ZERO, ZERO IS THE CENTER OF THE WORLD," said Harper. "It's also our original spawn point. And I believe . . ." She scanned their surroundings. From the hilltop, she could see a good distance. "Over there, by those trees. **THAT'S WHERE THIS ALL BEGAN."**

"And where it ends," Morgan said.

Po gulped audibly.

"For the Evoker King, I mean," Morgan added quickly. "I'm sure *we'll* be fine. . . ."

Harper led the way down the hill and **toward their spawn point.**

"We still don't even know what we're looking for," complained Morgan. **"THE SOURCE OF THE EVOKER KING'S POWER? IT COULD BE**

JUST ABOUT ANYTHING."

"It could be a unicorn!" said Jodi.

"Jodi . . . ," said Morgan.

"It could be!" she insisted. **"OR . . . OR A MAGICAL WISHING LAMP. WITH AN AI GENIE INSIDE."**

"Is it a tree?" asked Po. "Because I see a tree over there. And a tree over there. And not much else."

"It's underground," Harper said.

"What is?" asked Ash.

"The source of the Evoker King's power. **HE SAID IT WAS IN A DUNGEON."** She hopped up and down. "It must be beneath our feet!"

"The center of the world," said Ash. "In more ways than one . . ."

"Exactly," said Harper. She held up a pickaxe. "It's time to get digging."

Morgan put up a hand. **"ONE MINUTE. WE'RE SURE WE HAVE EVERYTHING WE NEED?** Everything from my list?"

Ash nodded. "Between the treasure chests

full of supplies that the Librarian left for us . . . and the stuff we made with resources from the Overworld and the Nether . . . yes." She smiled. **"WE'VE GOT ARMOR FOR EVERYONE, ENCHANTED WEAPONS, TONS OF FOOD, AND MORE BLAZE POWDER AND POTIONS THAN I'VE EVER SEEN IN ONE PLACE."**

"The trick is staying organized," said Po. "I don't want to be waving a fish around when I mean to use a sword."

Harper agreed. "He's got a point," she said. "Let's split everything up. **I'M ALREADY CARRYING ALL THE POTIONS. . . ."**

"And Ash has the best aim," Morgan said. "Maybe she should handle the arrows."

"Morgan is the boldest," said Jodi. "He should get the best armor and a shield."

"Oh wow," said Po. **"THIS IS JUST LIKE A FANTASY ADVENTURE!"**

"How do you mean?" Jodi asked.

"We're all choosing traditional fantasy hero roles. Morgan sounds like a fighter, or even a

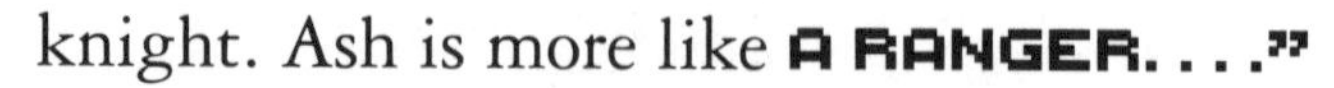

knight. Ash is more like **A RANGER. . . .”**

“I’m **AN ALCHEMIST,**” said Harper. “I can use potions to hurt our enemies and to heal us.”

“You’re like **A ROGUE,** Jodi,” said Po. “Sneaky and clever. And I can finally use my wizard skin again. Oh!” His eyes went wide. **“WHY DON’T WE ALL WEAR NEW SKINS TO FIT OUR ROLES?”**

“I don’t know,” said Morgan. “I’m not sure it’s the best use of our time.”

“Come on!” said Po. “It’ll make all the danger seem less . . . dangerous.”

"I don't see why not," said Jodi. Harper could tell she was already thinking of her new skin.

Ash shrugged, clearly warming up to the idea.

Harper smiled. **Po's enthusiasm was infectious.** "It might even be fun," she said.

Po's avatar blinked out of existence for the briefest of moments. Suddenly, where a human fly had just stood, there was a magical wizard in robes and a pointy hat.

"PO THE WIZARD," he said. "Ready to vanquish evil!"

Harper watched as her friends took a moment to adjust their looks.

"SIR MORGAN," said Morgan, hefting his shield. **"THE KNIGHT."**

Ash gripped her bow. **"ASH THE RANGER."**

"Jodi the . . . what was it?" She crouched, ready to pounce. "Oh, right. **JODI THE ROGUE!"**

Harper held up a flask. **"AND I'M ALCHEMIST HARPER**—potions prodigy and mistress of mixology." She grinned. "And I'm ready to conquer this dungeon."

Everyone cheered, eager for their adventure.

Chapter 5

THE DUNGEON WELCOMING COMMITTEE DESERVES ZERO STARS FROM A DISAPPOINTED VISITOR.

Morgan and his friends dug only for a minute before they found the start of a cavern.

There was a large underground hollow just beneath their feet. They descended carefully, carving out one block step at a time. It was dark. Even when they placed torches on the walls, they could see just a short distance. A tunnel stretched out before them, the ground sloping downward.

"IT SEEMS LIKE WE'RE ON THE RIGHT PATH," said Ash.

"Yeah," said Jodi. "The creepy, treacherous, descending-into-the-darkness, who-knows-what-could-be-down-there path. That seems right."

"FEAR NOT, BOLD ROGUE," said Po. "For we have magic on our side."

Jodi rolled her eyes, but she smiled.

"Our choice is clear," said Harper. "We need to push forward and hope for the best."

Morgan didn't know *what* to hope for. **He was wearing a full set of diamond armor**—the best armor possible! So he was less vulnerable than ever before.

But his friends and sister were plenty vulnerable. Did he have what it took to protect them all? That was the role of the person with the best armor. In gaming terms, he was the tank. And it was a big responsibility. **He shivered with uncertainty.**

Po leaned over and whispered in his ear. **"I'LL BET ALL THE MOBS WE ENCOUNTER DOWN HERE WILL BE WEARING CHICKEN COSTUMES,"** he said. "So there's nothing to be nervous about."

Morgan turned and gave his friend a grateful smile. Then he took a deep breath, gripped

his shield tight, and stepped forward.

The darkness gave way before them. Harper and Ash were right at Morgan's back, placing torches every few feet. Not only did that help them see, it would also help them retrace the route to their starting point.

After a few minutes, the dirt walls and floor became stone, and the tunnel opened up. Morgan had a sense that the space was large, but he could only see so far.

"I NEED MORE LIGHT," he said, so Harper held up a torch.

Morgan had been correct. They were in a vast cavern. But it wasn't made of rock and dirt, as he had expected. It was all stone and brick.

And there were little specks of red light sprinkled through the darkness.

"Spiders!" he hissed in warning.

"Then our foe has made a grave error," Po said in his wizard voice. "For we are smiters of spiders!

WE ARE ANNIHILATORS OF ARACHNIDS! We are—"

An arrow flew from the darkness. It narrowly missed Po, hitting the wall beside his head.

"WE ARE IN A LOT OF TROUBLE!" he cried.

The spiders emerged from the darkness. There were a dozen of them, and they weren't alone. Sitting atop each spider was a skeleton. The bony creatures were armed with bows and arrows, and they were aiming them right at Morgan and his friends.

Spider jockeys!

Po screamed.

Jodi ducked into the shadows. Harper and Ash hurried to replace their torches with weapons.

"Come and get me, you ghouls!" Morgan shouted to get the attention of their foes.

He sounded braver than he felt. But this was the tank's job, wasn't it? Every arrow that he blocked was an arrow that wasn't going to hurt one of his friends.

He held his shield up and ran toward the spider jockeys.

If his hope was to get their attention, then it worked. The spiders all moved toward him. **The skeletons all fired in his direction.** As long as they were right in front of him, he could block the arrows with his shield.

But soon he would be surrounded. There was no way he could fight them all.

Not alone . . .

A spider jockey just ahead of him was hit with a flask. The container exploded on impact, covering both spider and skeleton with a sickly green poison.

"Yes!"

cried Harper. **“DIRECT HIT!”**

Another skeleton was knocked off its spider by a well-placed arrow. The spider didn’t seem bothered—but soon it, too, was pelted with arrows.

“GOT ’EM!” yelled Ash as she prepared to let another arrow fly.

Two more spiders burst into flame as if they’d been hit with blazing fireballs. Their skeletal riders went flying.

“Woo-hoo!” cried Po.

Morgan heard a small voice say, **“AND WHILE YOU ALL ARE MAKING A RACKET . . .”**

Suddenly Jodi leapt from the shadows. **“SNEAK ATTACK!”** she hissed. She sped toward the skeletons who had lost their spiders in the fireball, slashing them from behind. By the time the skeletons turned to fight back, she was gone.

Morgan took advantage of the distraction, finishing off both skeletons with his sword.

He turned to face the next foe. To his surprise, every skeleton jockey was already defeated.

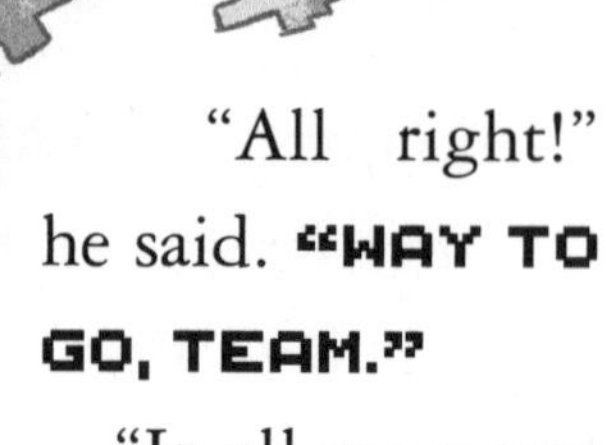

"All right!" he said. **"WAY TO GO, TEAM."**

"In all my many centuries of life, I never saw a finer fellowship," said Po. He was standing on top of a dispenser block.

"IS THAT HOW YOU SHOT THE FIREBALL?" Morgan asked.

Po nodded. "Fire charges and a dispenser," he said. "I know it's not an actual fireball spell, but it's close enough."

"It certainly took care of those things," Jodi said, stepping from the shadows. **"IT WAS EVEN MORE EFFECTIVE THAN MY SNEAK ATTACK."**

"I'm glad everyone's feeling good about this," said Harper.

"Me too," said Ash. "But that was only the first challenge. **AND WHO KNOWS HOW DEEP THIS PLACE GOES?"** She held up a torch, and the kids took in the size of the room. It was huge, and it was *constructed*—built of stonework and columns, not simply carved out in the dirt.

Morgan and Ash shared a look. He could tell she had the same worry he did.

There were dungeons in Minecraft. Morgan had seen plenty of them. But they were small underground caves. **Nothing like this.**

Someone had built this. And they'd put those spider jockeys here to guard it.

There would surely be greater threats ahead.

"If this place goes much deeper, we're bound to run out of torches," said Harper. "We should use them more sparingly."

Jodi pulled something from her inventory. "We can use my seed trick!" she said. "If we leave a trail of seeds behind us, we won't get lost. **THEN WE CAN AVOID WASTING TORCHES."**

"That's a good idea," said Morgan. "We'll take it slow. We'll check every nook and cranny of this place. And after we've got what we're looking for, we'll follow the seed trail back out again."

"EVERYBODY READY?" said Ash. Harper

had looted the fallen spider jockeys, and Po had reclaimed his dispenser.

"Ready," said Jodi.

"Follow close, everyone," said Morgan. He took a step deeper into the cavern. "We don't want to get—"

There was a *click.*

Morgan had just enough time to think, *It's a trap!*

And then the floor opened up beneath their feet, and they went tumbling into the darkness.

Chapter 6

THE OL' TRAPDOOR TRICK . . . I CAN'T BELIEVE THEY FELL FOR THAT.

Ash couldn't even find her voice to scream.

She was in complete free fall. She reached out, but there was nothing to hold on to. Nothing to slow her fall at all.

And no way to tell what awaited her below.

"HAAALP!" cried Po.

"Somebody do something!" yelled Jodi.

So it wasn't just *her* falling. **Her friends were there, too.** Ash wasn't sure whether that made it better or worse.

Then someone accidentally kicked her in the face. *It's worse,* she decided. *Definitely worse.*

She braced herself for impact. There had to be an end to this fall eventually. And it was going to *hurt.*

But when Ash finally stopped, there wasn't any pain. She heard a loud *slap,* and her fall slowed, until she was . . . drifting.

Water, she thought. *Thank goodness. We landed in water!*

She was relieved, but the feeling didn't last. Her momentum had carried her below the water's

surface. **It was pitch-black down there,** and she'd lost all sense of direction. She could only hold her breath for so long. Which way was up?

She saw a dim light out of the corner of her eye. It was coming from a strange-shaped block, more of a small rectangle than a cube. . . .

A sea pickle!

Po was placing a colony of sea pickles on the stony ground below. They gave off just enough light for Ash to get her bearings. She swam upward, and saw that the others were doing the same.

Po was the last one to burst through the surface. Ash could barely see him, but **she heard him gasping for air.**

"Po, you mad genius," she said. "I can't believe you had sea pickles in your inventory this whole time."

"I can't believe you didn't," said Po. "Sea pickles are the best."

"SAVED BY SEA PICKLES," said Harper. "I never would have believed it."

"Where are we?" asked Jodi. Her voice echoed in the dark.

"It must be some kind of underground reservoir," said Ash. "*Very* underground. **WE WERE FALLING FOR A LONG TIME. . . .**"

"I think I see the shore," Morgan said. "That way."

Together they swam to a small stretch of sand. The sand bar was wedged between the water and a sheer stone wall.

"THERE'S NO WAY WE CAN CLIMB OUT," Jodi said.

Harper peered upward. "We could build a staircase, but it would take some time. We may be better off digging through the wall."

"Tomorrow," Ash said. "Anything might be waiting for us on the other side of it, and we just had a very close call."

"You're right," Harper agreed. **"WE SHOULD REGROUP. EAT SOME FOOD, SET UP OUR BEDS . . ."**

"Ooh," said Po. "Dungeon camping. It could be a new trend."

"Anyway, it must be getting late," said Ash. She turned to Morgan. **"AND YOU STILL HAVE**

TO MEMORIZE YOUR LINES FOR THE PLAY."

In the darkness, she heard Morgan chuckle nervously.

At school the next day, Ash felt like she was in free fall all over again.

There was just so much to *do.*

As stage manager, **she was expected to keep an eye on every aspect of the play.** The actors, the sets, the props, light and sound—she was responsible for keeping *all* of it on track.

To make matters more complicated, this was a play no one had ever staged before. Ms. Minerva had wanted the students to do *The Phantom of the Opera,* a famous musical based on a famous book, but she hadn't been able to get permission, so she had written a new play, all by herself. It was called *The Phantasm of the Cafetorium,* and much like their teacher herself, it was kooky. Ms. Minerva seemed to have combined the story of

Phantom of the Opera with her own love for French pastries. "Creative people must look for inspiration everywhere!" she'd said.

In fact, Ms. Minerva had encouraged students **to look for inspiration in their own hobbies and interests.** Harper, who was in charge of the props, had taken that advice to heart. **She'd decided to give her creations a blocky Minecraft twist.**

"Remind you of anything?" Harper asked when Ash came by to check on her. She held up a rectangular box about the size of her forearm. She squeezed it, and one end glowed bright red.

Ash gasped. "It looks just like a **redstone torch!**" she said.

Even Baron Sweetcheeks seemed impressed. The hamster poked his head out of Ash's shirt pocket to get a closer look at the glowing red prop.

"Looking to Minecraft for inspiration has given my whole team a ton of ideas," Harper said. **"And the Phantasm's underground**

lair needed a light source."

Ash was glad that Harper and her team were letting their imaginations run wild. But there was one rule they had to follow. . . .

"Harper," Ash said. "That thing isn't high-tech, is it?"

Harper shook her head. **"It's basically a flashlight.** Just a battery and a few wires. No computer parts at all."

Ash breathed a sigh of relief. **Their school's technology had recently gone haywire** and caused all kinds of problems. Only Ash and her friends knew the reason: the school's tech had been invaded by the Evoker King. **He had caused glitches and malfunctions in pretty**

much anything that was plugged in.

That threat was over, and everything had gone back to normal at Woodsword. But Ms. Minerva refused to take any chances on the show. Low-tech was the order of the day.

"Good work," Ash said. **"But you should start on the fake croissants soon."**

"I don't get it," Harper said, rubbing her chin. "*Why* does the Phantasm like croissants so much?"

"Well, it's a love/hate thing," Ash explained. **"He blames croissants for the deaths of his parents,** so he *wants* to hate them. But they taste so buttery and delicious, so . . ."

Harper gave her a blank look.

"It's a weird script," Ash admitted. "But we're going to make the best of it."

Ash checked on Jodi's team next. They were in charge of painting backdrops for the set. They'd started with the Phantasm's lair.

"Looks great, Jodi!" Ash said, taking in the gray stone and ivy-covered columns. "Our recent dungeon crawl has given you some inspiration."

"It sure has," Jodi agreed. She scratched her

head. "But there's one thing I don't get. Why does the Phantasm stash all his stolen croissants underground? **Shouldn't he just eat them?"**

"Because I hate them," said a voice.

Ash and Jodi turned to see their classmate **Theo.** He was wearing **a black cape** and speaking with a strange accent.

"I hate them," he said, his eyes blazing with intensity. "And yet . . . how can I? **They are so buttery and delicious. . . ."** He smiled. "So?" The accent was gone. "What do you think?"

"Sounding good, Theo," said Ash. "And looking good, too!"

Theo had been cast as the Phantasm. He had the most lines of any of the actors, but Ash wasn't worried about Theo's ability to memorize them—he seemed to be a natural. Unlike some others in the cast . . .

"Hey, did I hear you

say something about **a dungeon delve?"** Theo asked. "What game are you playing these days?"

Jodi stepped forward. "Oh . . . a little bit of this, a little bit of that," she said. Ash didn't really get it, but **some of her friends didn't fully trust Theo.** He'd had a misunderstanding with Harper a while back, and **Morgan had even thought Theo might actually be the Evoker King.** But they knew that wasn't true now, and Ash was ready to let bygones be bygones.

Even so, she knew that the details of their Minecraft adventures needed to be kept secret. What if their teachers learned **the truth about what the VR headsets** could do? Ash found it hard to imagine they'd let the kids continue to use such amazing technology for gaming. So the fewer people who knew, the better. And unfortunately, that included Theo.

Baron Sweetcheeks squeaked, and Ash remembered she still had a lot to do.

"Keep up the good work, everyone," she said, and she moved on.

Po wasn't at the lighting controls, as she

expected. Instead, he was backstage, holding a copy of the script while Morgan practiced his lines.

"Unhand that donut!" Morgan said.

"Okay, good emotion that time," said Po. "But it's 'croissant.' "

"Right," said Morgan. "Okay. I've got it this time." He cleared his throat and threw his shoulders back. **"Dehand that croissant!"**

"Okay, pretty good," said Po. "*Dehand* is definitely not a word, but otherwise—"

"Po!" said Ash. **"Why aren't you figuring out the lights?"**

Po held up his copy of the script. It was all marked up with handwriting, highlights, and sticky notes. **"Already done, Captain.** I've got it all figured out, and all my cues are written down in my script." He inclined his head toward Morgan. "So I offered to help Morgan run his lines."

"I need the help," Morgan said, rubbing the back of his head. "Remembering all these lines doesn't comes naturally to me."

"You'll get there," said Po.

Ash gave Po a warm, appreciative smile.

She knew he would have liked an acting part, if only his basketball schedule hadn't made that impossible. **But instead of taking out his disappointment on others, he was doing everything he could to help.**

And then, over Po's shoulder, Ash caught a glimpse of the other person who hadn't been given the role she wanted. It was **Doc Culpepper,** their science teacher. She was watching all the activity unfold without her. **From the slump of her shoulders, Ash knew the teacher felt left out.**

But Ms. Minerva hadn't just banned high-tech equipment. When Doc had approached Ms. Minerva with ideas for upgrading the lights and sound system for the play, Ms. Minerva had said no. She'd forbidden Doc to touch *any* equipment that would be used in the play.

Ash understood where Ms. Minerva was coming from. Doc's upgrades often caused as many problems as they solved. **And it was her tinkering that had given the Evoker King access to the school's systems.**

But Ash hated to see anyone disappointed. She turned in Doc's direction, determined to find some way to include the teacher. **But then Morgan flubbed another line,** and Ash realized she had her hands full already.

By the time she thought about it again, **Doc was already gone.**

Chapter 7

THE FLOOR IS LAVA! ALSO, THE WALLS ARE LAVA! OH MAN, EVERYTHING IS LAVA!!

As soon as they returned to the game, **Harper hefted her pickaxe.**

If they were right, the object they wanted would be found deep belowground. So there was no point trying to go back up to the room where **they'd fought the spider jockeys.** Instead, they would hack their way through the stone wall at the water's edge.

Harper expected to find more darkness on the other side. Instead, the air radiated with **an orange-red tint.** She knew what that meant before she'd even stepped through the narrow tunnel they'd cut.

"LAVA," Jodi said breathlessly. "I've never seen so much of it."

Harper hadn't either. **A great expanse of lava stretched out below them,** like an ocean of roiling fire. More lava streamed down from high above, **forming awe-inspiring lavafalls.** The gray stone of the bridge they stood on looked orange in the glow of the cavern. More bridges crisscrossed the space. There were bridges above them, bridges below them, bridges running in every direction. They formed a complex set of walkways—it was hard to imagine where they all led. Harper felt dizzy trying to take it all in. And she knew those bridges were the only surfaces that would be safe to touch. **Touching lava, on the other hand, would be a very bad idea.**

"We'll have to be careful," she warned. "One false step . . ."

"Please don't finish that sentence," said Po.

"WE'LL STAY ON THE BRIDGE," Jodi said. "Right in the middle of the bridge. Honest."

If even Jodi and Po were taking this seriously, then Harper knew she was right to be worried.

They followed the bridge to a crossroads. **They**

could choose any of three directions.

"How do we know which way?" asked Morgan.

"Without any information to go on, one guess is as good as any other," said Harper. **"EENY, MEENY, LET'S GO THAT WAY."**

They turned right, following the stone walkway until it ended at a wall.

"Should we cut through the wall?" asked Jodi.

"IT'S AWFULLY RISKY," said Ash. "For all we know, there's more lava on the other side, just waiting to rush in."

"I think I see where we need to go," said Po. He pointed over the edge of the bridge. **"CHECK THAT OUT."**

Harper peered over the ledge, taking care not to get too close. Po was right. Below them, at the level of the lava, **there was a red door.** It was the only door in sight. Surely it would lead them **deeper into the dungeon.**

Harper tried to trace the path that would lead them to the door. But there were too many bridges and strange intersections. **It was impossible to follow the path with her eyes.**

"It's a maze," she said. "A three-dimensional maze suspended over a vast sea of lava."

"And I thought memorizing dialogue was tough," said Morgan.

"Forget the maze," said Po. **"WE CAN BUILD OUR OWN BRIDGE FROM HERE."**

"Hmm." Ash tapped her chin. "We didn't bring enough building material with us."

"BUT I SUPPOSE WE COULD DISMANTLE THIS BRIDGE AND REASSEMBLE IT," Harper said, finishing Ash's thought.

"I don't love the idea of moving blocks around when those blocks are the only thing keeping us from, you know . . . *fwoosh!*" Morgan said.

"WE'LL BE CAREFUL," Harper promised.

Jodi grinned. “Why be careful when you can be creative?”

“Spoken like a true rogue,” Po said in his wizard voice. “Tell us, then, young ruffian. What trick do you have in mind?”

“AND SPOIL THE SURPRISE?” Jodi said. “Just follow me, Po the Wise, and maybe I’ll teach you something new.”

They followed Jodi, retracing their steps to the hole they’d cut through the wall.

“WE’RE BACK WHERE WE STARTED,” Morgan complained.

Jodi didn’t say anything. Instead of returning to the reservoir room, she walked to the edge of the bridge, right where it met the wall. **Then she started placing blocks, forming a ledge that would allow her to walk along the wall.**

Po peered at the lava below. "I thought this was exactly what we wanted to avoid."

"Don't worry," Jodi said. "This is as close to the lava as I'm going to get." She'd built her narrow walkway so that she now stood a little bit below the level of the bridge. "Anybody want to guess what's on the other side of this wall?" She tapped the stone beside her.

"Ah," said Ash. **"I THINK I UNDERSTAND."**

"What?" said Morgan. "What's the plan?"

Harper caught on next. She laughed. "The reservoir. There's an enormous amount of water right in the other room! **AND WHAT HAPPENS WHEN YOU ADD WATER TO LAVA?"** she said.

Po stroked his beard. "Steam?"

"Not in Minecraft," Morgan said, at last understanding Jodi's plan. "In Minecraft, water and lava make—"

"COBBLESTONE," said Jodi. "One sidewalk, coming up!" And with that, she swung her pickaxe and hacked a hole through the wall.

Water rushed through the hole immediately, forming a small blue waterfall.

Harper and the others watched in awe as the water mixed with the lava below. In a matter of minutes, most of **the fiery sea had become a cobblestone floor,** perfectly safe to walk upon.

"Way to go, Jodi," said Po. **"THAT'S WHAT I CALL THINKING OUTSIDE THE BLOCKS!"**

But the lava maze was only the beginning of the challenges they faced that day. They encountered more skeletons, bats, zombies, and slimes, and **a creeper who almost blasted Morgan** right off a narrow walkway. They quaffed potions, **forged new weapons** to replace the old, and even stopped to collect riches and other materials they found along the way.

Their strategies worked better than Harper had dared to hope. She had a potion for every situation she could think of. Morgan faced their enemies head-on, while Jodi struck from the shadows. Po and Ash attacked from a safe distance, Ash with arrows and Po with his fireball dispenser. **The dispenser itself was**

a simple-looking block that reminded Harper of a furnace. But it was powered with redstone, and when Po filled the item with fire charges, it spat fire at their enemies. (Harper knew it would also launch snowballs, but she decided that wouldn't be much use to them here.)

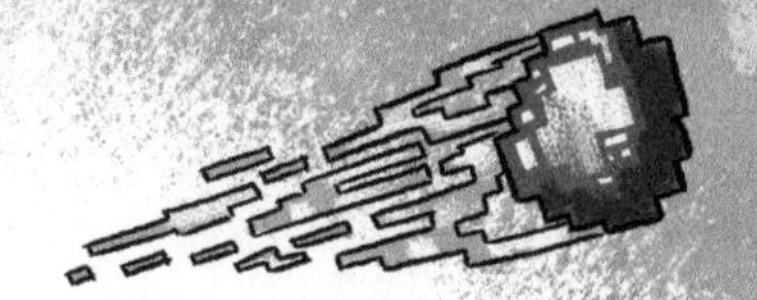

Together, the friends traveled through endless levels and still had food and healing potions to spare. And then they came to the bridge of light.

Unlike the stone walkways in the lava room, this bridge was a wide construction made entirely of glowstone. Harper had seen plenty of glowstone in its raw form in the Nether. But she'd never seen it put to use like this. She certainly hadn't expected such a sight **in the middle of a dark dungeon** miles underground.

Her friends clearly felt the same. They wore shocked expressions, their mouths hanging open in awe.

Harper checked her compass. "We're almost directly below our original spawn point," she said. "Coordinates zero, zero."

In the distance, at the far end of the bridge, she could just make out a huge, heavy door. It looked almost like a vault. "Whatever we're looking for . . . ," she said, "I think it's just ahead."

"Then why are we waiting?" said Morgan. **"LET'S GO!"**

They broke into a run. **Their goal was so close, Harper could taste it.**

But as they crested the bridge, **four shadowy figures** came into view.

"Who are they?" Ash whispered. She skidded to a stop, and the others stopped as well.

"Whoever they are, they're standing between us and victory," said Morgan.

"THEY MUST BE GUARDS," Po said. "Right? They're definitely here to keep us out."

"I think you're right," said Jodi. "I've got a bad feeling. . . ."

"Forget bad feelings," Harper said. They all turned to look at her. "We've come this far," she said. **"WE'VE FOLLOWED A PLAN, AND IT'S WORKED.** So I say we keep following the plan."

Po shrugged. "She's got a point. Why mess with a winning formula?"

"It'll be fine," said Morgan. **"JUST FOLLOW MY LEAD!"**

Morgan ran ahead, raising his sword and shield as he went.

One of the figures launched a barrage of arrows.

Arrows again, thought Harper, remembering the skeleton jockeys. *Nothing to worry about.*

But she was wrong. Though Morgan hollered and waved his sword and did everything he could to attract their foes' attention, the arrows weren't aimed at him.

The arrows were aimed at the rest of them.

"TAKE COVER!" yelled Ash.

"Where?!" cried Po. "We're sitting ducks on this bridge!"

Harper agreed, but she didn't waste breath saying so. She ran back and forth, **desperate to avoid the arrows.**

One of the four figures stepped out of the gloom. The figure was mounted on some kind of animal. Harper expected another spider jockey. Or worse.

But what she saw was unlike anything she'd seen before.

The female figure was a knight. Her armor looked a little bit like Morgan's. But where his armor gleamed bright in the light of the glowstone, hers was dark as a starless night. She rode a four-legged reptile. It was the size of a horse, but **it looked like a dragon,** with gleaming yellow eyes and sinister teeth.

"That's not . . . ," said Morgan. "That's not possible."

"What is it?!" cried Jodi.

"IT DOESN'T EXIST IN MINECRAFT," said Ash. "It doesn't belong here."

As if angered by Ash's statement, the creature tilted its head and roared.

"Retreat!" cried Harper, realizing that escape was necessary in the face of this unknown threat. **"EVERYONE, FALL BACK!"**

They retreated the full length of the bridge, dodging arrows the whole way. When they reached the previous room, they shut the door behind them, then barricaded it with obsidian for good measure.

"WE'VE GOT TO GET OUT OF HERE," Ash said. "We need to come back with a plan for how to deal with . . . whatever that was."

"Let's carve out a cave off the main path," Morgan said. "We can cover our tracks. Make a hideout inside the walls where they can't find us."

"SOUNDS COZY," said Po.

"Sounds *necessary,*" said Harper. All the confidence she'd felt just minutes ago had left her. "It looks like the Evoker King has upped his game." She paused. **"AND WE'D BETTER HOPE WE'RE GOOD ENOUGH TO BEAT HIM."**

Chapter 8

THERE'S NO SUCH THING AS AN UNWANTED COOKIE.

Throughout the school day, **Po kept thinking back to their encounter in the dungeon.** What should they have done differently? How would they ever reach that door when their path was blocked by an evil knight on a fearsome dragon? And what would they find if they *did* get through that door?

But he didn't have much time to dwell on it. **It was a game day for his basketball team,** and game days were always busy. Every kid he passed in the hallway extended their hand for a high five. (It was supposed to be good luck.) Several of the cheerleaders had brought the team

home-baked cookies, and he nibbled on them between classes. **(Tony's were the best!)** And there was a short pep rally right at the end of lunch period, where everybody sang the school song. (Well, almost everybody. Po knew that Morgan only pretended to sing, which was for the best.)

Po appreciated the support. He certainly liked the attention. But it felt a bit hollow today. **He knew most of his classmates would be staying at Woodsword for rehearsal**

tonight, while Po traveled to another school for the game. He felt like he was missing the main event.

But he was happy for the free cookies. He'd never turn *those* down.

At his locker after school, Harper and Ash stopped by to wish him luck.

"I wish I could stay here and help you with the play," he said.

"Forget it," said Ash. "The lighting cues you wrote in your script are perfect. **Someone else will be able to run the lights for one rehearsal."**

"And your team needs you!" Harper added.

Po smiled. **He knew they wanted to help him stay focused on the game.** But he wished that the play needed him, too.

"Hey, Ash," said a voice, and **they turned to see Theo approaching.** When he saw Harper standing there, he grew suddenly awkward.

"Oh. Hi, Harper. Nice to see you."

"Nice to see you, too," said Harper shyly. The two hadn't really spent any time together since having a big disagreement a few months before. **Theo had sabotaged the coral restoration project that the two of them had worked on.** And although he'd had good intentions, Harper had been hurt by his actions.

Theo turned back to Ash. "Ms. Minerva asked me to find you," he said. "She says she has some new ideas and **might rewrite the ending.**"

Ash's face flushed, and she clenched her fists. **"The answer is no!"** she said. "The script is set. We can't keep changing things!"

Theo stepped back. "Don't blame the messenger," he said.

"Take a breath, Ash," added Po.

"No time!" she said. They watched as **she stormed off**

toward the auditorium.

Harper turned to follow her. "Good luck, Po," she said. "Bye, Theo!"

Theo rubbed the back of his head. "Hey, Po, you're in charge of the lights for the play, right?" he said. **"I had some ideas for how to automate them. It might make your job easier, and it's a simple program. . . ."**

Po shook his head. "No can do, buddy," Po said. "Ms. Minerva might keep changing her mind about the ending, but **she's one hundred percent against going high-tech."**

"Oh well," said Theo. "I figured it was worth asking. I'll get to show off my programming skills one day. . . . Anyway, good luck tonight!"

"Thanks," said Po. And once Theo had left, he realized the hallway had cleared out. **He needed to get to the bus.** But he looked longingly over his shoulder, in the direction of the auditorium, where laughter and music echoed.

Chapter 9

KEEP YOUR HEAD IN THE GAME! BUT IMAGINING YOU'RE A WIZARD IS OKAY, TOO.

Po's thoughts were being pulled in a half dozen directions. He was thinking about the play. He was worrying about **the sinister guardians** of the glowstone bridge. And he was wondering what **the source of the Evoker's King power** actually was.

With all that on his mind, it probably shouldn't have been a surprise when Po made a mistake on the court. What should have been an easy block went wrong, and the referee hit him with a penalty.

With their free throws, **the other team took the lead.**

"Keep your head in the game, Po!" yelled his coach. Po didn't like being called out like that. Especially when the coach was right. **Po needed to focus on one thing at a time.**

Then again, Po felt he was often at his best when he let his imagination run wild. **It was one of the reasons he enjoyed trying out new skins in Minecraft.** With each skin, he became a different character. Those characters were often bold, fearless—so that even when Po himself was afraid, he could pretend to be someone who wasn't.

Surely the great mage Po the Wise would not be bested at basketball. In his mind, the wizard flew across the court, covering yards in mere seconds. Po approached the

basket. The wizard was suddenly surrounded by fierce opponents.

The wizard smiled. Po passed the ball to his teammate Raul. The horde rushed the wizard too late. **Raul made a heroic three-point shot.**

That was something else Po the Wise knew well. Teamwork was a real-life superpower.

"Attaboy, Po!" said Coach. **"There's my star."**

Normally, Po would have loved hearing that. Tonight, it made his stomach twist.

Po's basketball team was **a mixed-ability wheelchair team.** That meant the team played in wheelchairs, even though many of the players didn't use wheelchairs outside of the sport.

Po hadn't been able to use his legs since birth. But he'd always been active and energetic, and **he'd always hated being told he couldn't do something.** Po suspected the reason he'd fallen in love with wheelchair basketball in the first place was because some people assumed people with paraplegia couldn't be athletes.

Proving the doubters wrong? That

was just the sort of challenge Po relished. Po didn't want to be *just* a basketball player, however. **He wanted to try other things, too.**

Acting, for instance.

But the thought of telling his coach that he would miss some games for play rehearsal? The idea of telling his teammates that he wouldn't be there for them? The possibility of giving up all those high fives and cookies? Those things were difficult to imagine.

Po liked being a star. If he gave up basketball for something new, he would risk losing all he had.

At that moment, Raul passed Po the ball. **Po's head snapped back into the game.** He forgot about everything except the ball in his hands, the basket up ahead, and the friends and teammates all around him.

"Po, you were amazing!" said Jodi.

"Oh, yeah," Morgan said. **"Good game, buddy."**

It had been a really close game, in fact, but Woodsword had managed the win. Friends and family had swarmed the court after the game clock hit zero. Po hadn't even realized that Morgan and Jodi were in the bleachers.

"You two skipped play practice?" he asked.

"The set-design team is ahead of schedule," Jodi said, beaming. "So I left early tonight."

Morgan shrugged. **"I'm still working on my part,"** he said. "But Ash said she had her hands full with other stuff, so I got the night off, too."

"Enough about *Phantasm,*" said Jodi. "We were talking about what a great player you are."

Po wanted to bask in the praise,

but he found he couldn't enjoy it. "Thanks," he said. "But I don't know. . . . There's more to life than basketball."

"What are you even saying right now?" said Morgan. He laughed. "What kind of talk is that from **the guy who just won the game?"**

Jodi tilted her head to one side and gave Po a long, searching look. "He's not wrong, big brother," she said. "There *is* more to life than basketball."

"Tomorrow, maybe. Right now?" He ruffled Po's hair. "Right now this is all that matters. **You should revel in your victory, Po!"**

"Yeah!" Po replied. "You're right." And he tried to do just what Morgan suggested. He put on a smile for his friends and acted goofy for his teammates.

But his mind was still elsewhere, chasing phantasms.

Chapter 10

INTRODUCING . . . BLOCK PARTY! THEY'LL KNOCK YOUR BLOCK OFF!

"We're in agreement, then?" Ash asked her friends. **Their expressions were as thoughtful and serious** as their block faces could be.

"Our strategy got us this far," said Morgan. "It just has to work one more time."

"They turned us away before," said Harper. **"BUT THIS TIME, WE'RE READY."**

"Yeah," said Po. "This time, when I see the dragon beast, I'll only scream *a little.*"

Jodi elbowed him. "We're all in agreement, Ash," she said.

Obsidian didn't break easily. It took

time to remove their barrier. As Harper chipped away at it with a diamond pickaxe, Ash felt a flash of nervousness.

We are *ready,* she told herself. *We can't have come this far only to fail.*

Once the barrier was down, the glow of the bridge shone bright. **Ash had to shield her eyes** from the glare as she stepped from darkness into light. When her vision adjusted, she saw those same figures standing on the bridge, just a short distance ahead.

"Right where we left them," Po whispered. **"LIKE THEY'RE WAITING FOR US . . ."**

This time, Ash got a good look at them. Standing there beside **the dark knight and her dragon mount** was the strangest group of mobs she had ever seen. There was a fierce-looking zombie wielding an ax. There was a scruffy-looking sailor with a crossbow. And, finally, there was a robed, hooded figure with a bow.

"What *are* they?" Morgan asked under his breath. "Are they . . . are they people, like us?"

"ARE YOU FELLOW GAMERS? MAYBE WE

COULD BE FRIENDS?" tried Jodi.

The sailor opened his mouth to respond. But his voice came out as a honk.

The mobs all started honking then. They sounded just like mindless villagers.

"I don't think they're people . . . ," said Harper.

"AND I DON'T THINK THEY'RE FRIENDLY!" Po cried out as the strange quartet went on the attack.

"Jodi!" said Ash. "Go invisible. Try to get behind them."

"You've got it," said Jodi. **She downed a potion of invisibility in a single gulp,** and Ash watched as she faded from view.

"Everyone else, stay behind me," said Morgan. **He planted his feet firmly on the bridge** and held up his sword.

Ash drew her bow. **She**

nodded at Harper, who was preparing to throw a potion.

But before the girls could attack, the dark knight barreled forward. She ignored Morgan completely, steering her dragon around him, keeping just out of reach of his sword.

"NO FAIR!" said Morgan, swinging his sword and hitting only empty air. "I'm the tank! Fight me!"

While Morgan's attention was on the knight, two more of the figures slipped past him. **The zombie and the sailor seemed to think better of attacking the well-armored warrior.** They were headed right for Ash and Harper.

But the knight went after Po. She knocked him over before he'd had a chance to load his fireball dispenser.

And Po didn't have any other weapons.

Ash wanted to help him, but the zombie with the ax was right in her face. Armed only with a bow, **she was vulnerable to the creature's melee attacks.** She kept backing up, but before she could fire off a shot, he would lunge forward, closing the distance between them.

"I CAN'T SEE!" yelled Jodi.

Ash turned to look farther up the bridge, past Morgan. Jodi was visible again. She was on her knees beside the cloaked figure. **That mob was some kind of spellcaster.** Swirling black clouds streamed from his outstretched hands, engulfing Jodi in darkness.

"Our rogue is fighting blind," Harper said. **She lobbed exploding potions at the sailor,** who dodged them easily, coming closer with each passing moment.

"Jodi!" cried Morgan. **"HOLD ON, I'M COMING!"**

"Morgan, wait!" yelled Ash. He didn't listen, and Ash was struck by the zombie while her attention had been divided. Now Morgan and Jodi were on one side of the bridge, **Po was under attack** on the other, and Harper and Ash stood between them, unable to shake their own foes.

"OH, NO. We split the party. . . ."

"That's it!" Ash shouted. "Retreat! Everyone, fall back!" **She grabbed Harper, pulling her out of reach of the fighting-mad zombie and the agile sailor.**

"We can't get to you!" yelled Morgan. He was standing between the dark mage and his sister, blocking the spellcaster's arrows.

"PLAN B!" Ash said. "The potion Harper gave you earlier today. Everyone drink it and go!"

Ash watched to make sure everyone did as she'd told them. Morgan helped Jodi with her potion before drinking one himself. **Harper pulled Po away from the knight,** and they each

quaffed their own potions.

Ash drank hers then, and she ran toward the nearest edge of the bridge.

She ran right up to the edge. And she kept running, then **leapt off the bridge.**

Her stomach flipped. She half expected to plummet through the darkness like before. But the potion took effect, and instead of going into free fall, Ash floated down like a feather.

"THE POTION OF SLOW FALLING," she said. "Harper, it's working!"

She saw the others drifting downward nearby. Wherever they were going, they'd land safely.

An arrow whizzed by her head. Ash realized they weren't out of danger yet. Their enemies stood on the bridge, looking down at them and taking a few final shots.

"Heads up, everyone," she warned.

"THOSE GUYS ARE INTENSE," said Po. "I didn't even have time to grab my dispenser!"

"At least I can see again," said Jodi. "Well, sort of. It's awfully dark."

"I THINK I SEE THE GROUND JUST BELOW," said Morgan.

Morgan was right. **The stony floor rose to meet them,** and they all touched down gently at the same time. "Excellent job on the potions, Harper," said Po. "And did I detect just a hint of jasmine?"

Harper smirked. "If you tasted anything, it was probably the spider eyes."

Po made a horrified face.

"Hmm." Ash tapped her foot on the ground. "Bedrock," she said.

"I'm happy to be back on solid ground," said Jodi. **"BUT WHAT'S SPECIAL ABOUT BEDROCK?"**

"IT'S EVEN TOUGHER THAN OBSIDIAN," said Morgan. "In fact, it can't be mined at all. Otherwise you could make a hole right through the bottom of the world."

"So we're as far down as we can go, and it's a dead end," said Harper. **"WE NEED TO GET BACK UP TO THAT VAULT DOOR,** I think."

"How do we get past **THE BLOCK PARTY?"** Po asked. He turned to Jodi. "That's the amazing name I just came up with for our archenemies up there."

"Why doesn't our team have a name?" said Jodi.

"WE'RE TEAM PO," Po answered.

Everyone gave him a look.

He shrugged. "I thought everybody knew that already."

"Team Po might have met its match," Jodi said. "Those mobs anticipated our every move."

"What if this is as far as we can get?" Harper asked. **"WHAT IF WE CAN'T BEAT THEM?"**

"We'll think of something," Morgan said. "Right, Ash?"

Ash hesitated just a second too long before she said, "Of course."

Chapter 11

MANY HANDS MAKE LIGHT WORK. (LACKING THUMBS, MANY FEET TEND TO BE LESS USEFUL.)

The next day, **Po spent his lunch period in the auditorium.** Almost everybody did. There was a lot of work still to be done for the play, and there were only a few more days to do it all.

Po started by double-checking that the spotlights were ready to go. He had all his lighting cues firmly committed to memory. **And if he happened to forget anything, it was all clearly labeled in his script.** He would make sure the spotlight always followed whichever actor was speaking. And he knew to use the blue-tinted lights in the underground scenes, to make **everything look a little spookier.**

But other people were scrambling to get their own work done. So Po figured he could help.

Ash was grateful for the offer, and she handed him a big can of paint. "Can you please get this to Jodi's team?" she asked him. **"Tell her that's the last of the fuchsia!"**

"I don't know what that word means," said Po. "But consider it done."

On his way backstage to find Jodi, he ran into Morgan.

"Hey, Po, check it out!" Morgan said. **He held up a croissant.** It was angular, with pixelated edges. **It looked just like a food item from Minecraft.** "Mmm. . . . Doesn't it look good enough to eat?"

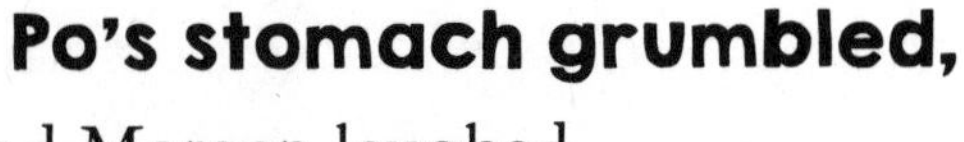

Po's stomach grumbled, and Morgan laughed.

"I guess that answers my question," Morgan said. "But

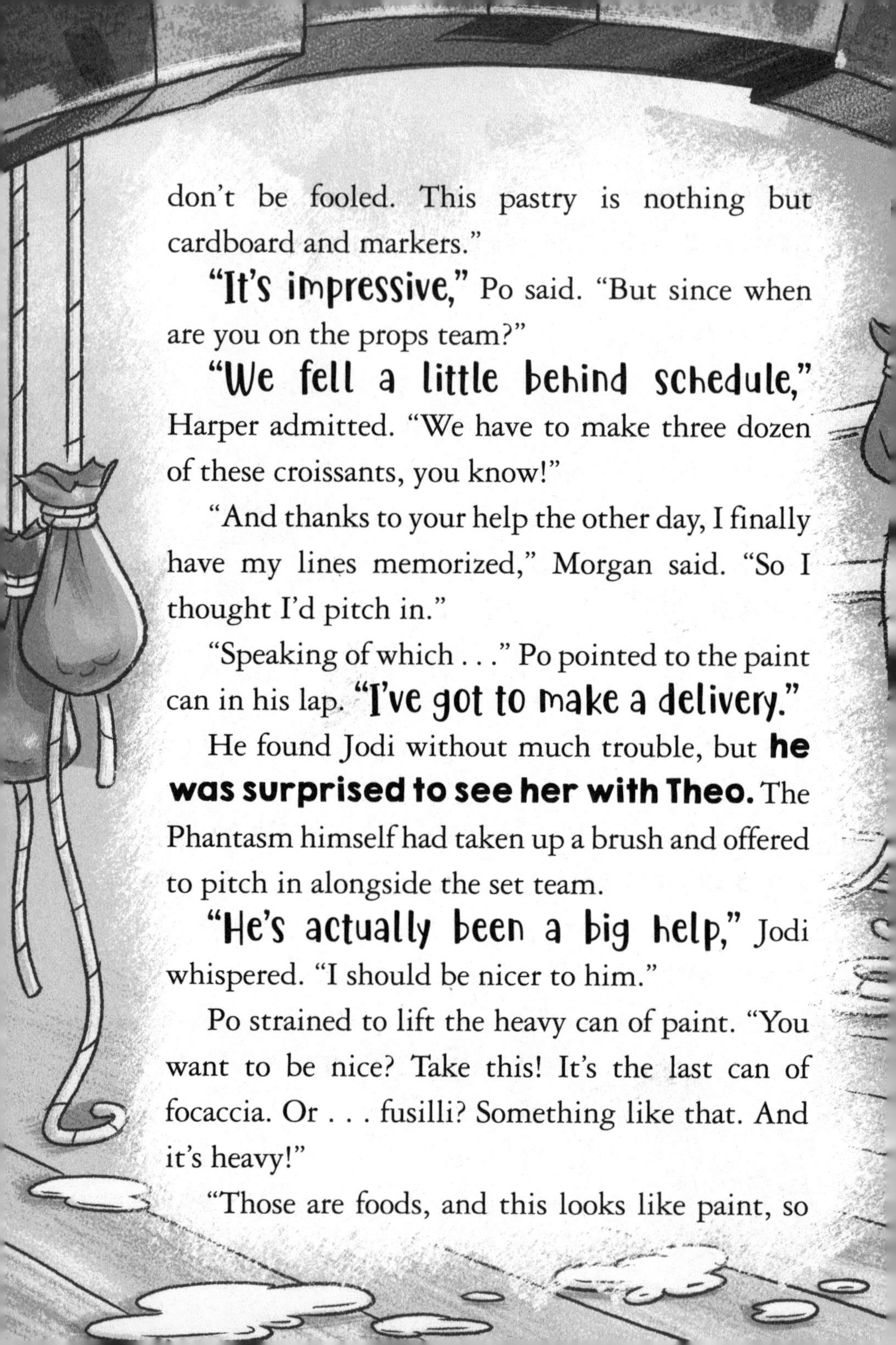

don't be fooled. This pastry is nothing but cardboard and markers."

"It's impressive," Po said. "But since when are you on the props team?"

"We fell a little behind schedule," Harper admitted. "We have to make three dozen of these croissants, you know!"

"And thanks to your help the other day, I finally have my lines memorized," Morgan said. "So I thought I'd pitch in."

"Speaking of which . . ." Po pointed to the paint can in his lap. **"I've got to make a delivery."**

He found Jodi without much trouble, but **he was surprised to see her with Theo.** The Phantasm himself had taken up a brush and offered to pitch in alongside the set team.

"He's actually been a big help," Jodi whispered. "I should be nicer to him."

Po strained to lift the heavy can of paint. "You want to be nice? Take this! It's the last can of focaccia. Or . . . fusilli? Something like that. And it's heavy!"

"Those are foods, and this looks like paint, so

HOOPS

I'm not sure what you're actually handing me right now." As she took the can from him, she looked all around. **"Say, have you seen Doc today?"** she asked. "I thought she was going to help. . . ."

"I'm pretty sure Ms. Minerva banned her," Po answered, "after she floated the idea of automated curtains."

"Ms. Minerva had better be careful!" Jodi said. **"Can't you just imagine Doc taking her revenge?** What if she's the true Phantasm? What terrible vengeance might she pursue?"

"You're right," Po said.

"I am?"

"Well, you're half right," he said. "I don't think Doc is going to swoop in here and take revenge on anybody. But we can find *something* for her to do, can't we?" He scratched his head. "Just because **she's the science and technology expert** doesn't mean she can *only* do science and technology stuff."

"We could find another role for her," Jodi agreed. "I'm sure we could."

And at that moment, it was as if a redstone switch clicked into place in Po's head. **"Eureka!"** he said.

He saw Ash walking by, and he reached out to grab her. Then he waved Harper and Morgan over.

Once they were all assembled, Po told his friends, "I've noticed something today. Even though everyone has a specific job on the play—a specific *role*—we don't stick to just that role. **We have to be flexible in order to help each other out."**

"And as stage manager, I appreciate it more than I can say," Ash said. Her eyes drifted to a nearby clock. "But do you have a point?"

"My point is that this is exactly what we're doing wrong in the dungeon. We—Oh, hey, Theo," Po said, noticing that the boy had slowly edged up to their circle.

Theo looked **momentarily guilty.** He cast his eyes around until they landed on the unopened can of paint at Jodi's feet. "Ah, there you are!" he said in his Phantasm voice. **"Just the very thing to satisfy my traitorous hunger!"**

Po smiled politely, and the others made room for Theo to come into their circle and grab the paint. **"I'm, uh, not really going to eat the paint,"** he said. "That's just a line from the play. Well, you all know that already. . . ."

Theo hesitated, clutching the paint to his chest.

He looked like he wanted to say something more, but **he gave a Phantasm-y farewell** and returned to his half-painted set.

"He's really getting into his role," said Ash. **"Good for him!"**

"Anyway," said Po, "as I was saying: We've been too rigid in the dungeon.

We've stuck to our roles almost too well. And that's made us totally predictable."

"It did seem like the **Block Party knew what to expect** from us," said Harper. "They tore through us where we were most vulnerable."

"The Evoker King must have set them on us," Morgan said. "He's probably been watching us the whole time. **He's desperate to stop us from finding the key to his power.** So desperate, he built entirely new mobs from scratch."

Ash narrowed her eyes. "I've been thinking about that, actually," she said. "Even though I'd never seen those mobs before, there was something **almost familiar about them."**

Morgan shrugged. "They're new to me. Although, the spellcaster with a bow reminded me of an illusionist. They use blindness spells, after all."

Ash snapped her fingers. "That's it! **The Block Party they're just illagers with different skins.** The one with the ax is a vindicator. The sailor with a crossbow is a pillager."

"What about the dragon?" Morgan asked.

"It's just a ravager with a fresh coat of paint!" Ash said, and at the mention of paint, Jodi waved her purple-drenched paintbrush.

"This is perfect," said Po. "This means we have a real advantage. We know what to expect from those NPCs, reskinned or not. **But they won't expect us to mix things up."**

Morgan grinned. **"I'm game."**

"Me too," said Jodi.

"I was tired of throwing potions around anyway," said Harper.

"Love it," said Ash. But her eyes were back on the clock. "Now, Morgan, **where are we on those croissants . . . ?"**

Chapter 12

TEAM PO VERSUS THE BLOCK PARTY (REMIX)! IN WHICH OUR NOBLE HEROES LAY DOWN THE SMACKDOWN!

Jodi was ready for their rematch.

They had set their beds up at the bottom of the pit, beneath a low stone ceiling that would hide them from view. **They broke through that ceiling now,** and Jodi could just barely see the glow of the bridge above.

High above. Jodi wished they could just cut through a wall, or somehow respawn back onto the bridge.

But they had a plan. A *real* plan this time. One that the Block Party wouldn't see coming.

And that plan relied on stealth. **They would sneak up on the guardian mobs.**

That meant building their way out of the pit, one block at a time.

Jodi hopped up and quickly placed a block of stone beneath her feet. She repeated the action, again and again, so that **a pillar of stone seemed to sprout right beneath her.** It was slow work, and she had to be careful to keep her balance. But she made steady progress—all of them did, each on their own pillar—and **they were perfectly silent as they ascended.**

In that way, they were all acting like rogues this time, getting into place for a sneak attack.

When the glowing bridge was within reach, **Jodi waited for Ash's signal.** Ash looked around, making sure everyone was ready. She raised her blocky fist, and they all leapt onto the bridge at the same time.

Their foes honked in surprise. Their stealthy approach had bought them a few precious seconds.

"EVERYONE BEHIND ME," Morgan said,

and **he stepped to the front again.** Just like the Block Party would expect. He still looked like a knight, after all.

But then he drank an invisibility potion and faded from view.

"SURPRISE, SUCKERS!" Jodi cried, and she pulled out a bow and let an arrow fly.

"Did you like that?" asked Harper. "Have another!" And she shot her own barrage of arrows into the crowd.

The Block Party had obviously been caught unprepared. **The sailor and the zombie were both struck by arrows.** They flashed red, a sure sign they'd taken damage.

"THE DRAGON IS MINE," said Po. "I owe it one!"

Po lobbed a green potion at the creature. The flask shattered on contact, **splashing the dragon with poison.** While the poison ate away at the creature's health, Po threw a dark blue potion at the dark knight. It was a splash potion of weakness, and it would make the knight's attacks far less deadly.

Before the knight could recover, Morgan stepped from the shadows and slashed her with his sword. **"SNEAK ATTACK!"** he said.

"And one more for good measure," said Po. He finished the false knight with a slash from his own sword. **Though he still wore his wizard skin, he was now outfitted with a few pieces of diamond armor.**

"The illusioner is down, too," said Ash. She stood over the fallen form of the dark mage, a shield in one hand and a diamond pickaxe in the other.

"That's all of them," said Po. **"WE DID IT!"**

Together they ran the length of the glowing bridge, coming to a stop just before the great door.

"You really think it's in there?" said Ash. **"THE**

KEY TO THE EVOKER KING'S POWER?"

Morgan rubbed his blocky hands together. "I say it's time to find out."

"Okay," said Jodi. "Go ahead, Morgan. Open the—"

In an instant, everything changed. **The blocks all around them broke into pixels,** and the pixels swirled and swelled. A light bloomed in Jodi's vision, and when she reached up to cover her eyes, **she felt . . . goggles.**

She was back in the computer lab.

Back in the real world.

"Door," she said.

"What was that?" Po asked, removing his goggles. **"WHAT JUST HAPPENED?!"**

"THE POWER'S COMPLETELY OFF," said Harper. She toggled a power switch. "The computers, they're all dead."

"OOPS!" said a voice. "I think that's my fault."

They all turned to see Theo standing there in the middle of the computer lab.

"I'm sorry, everybody," he said. "I was trying not to interrupt you, but I tripped on a cable. **I think I might have pulled out the main power plug."**

"We have to go back!" said Morgan. "We were so close!"

Ash shook her head. She pointed to the window. "It's already dark out. By the time we boot everything back up, it'll be too late."

"What were you even doing here, Theo?" asked Harper.

"I was looking for something I left in here earlier," he said. He cast his eyes about the room.

"Ah, there you are!" he said with his phony Phantasm accent. **"Just the very thing to satisfy my traitorous hunger!"**

He picked up a piece of paper. From where Jodi was sitting, it looked like just a **blank sheet of paper.**

"*That's* what you forgot in here?" Jodi asked. "Are you sure?"

"Farewell!" Theo cried, and he turned on his heel. If he'd been wearing his cape, it would have snapped dramatically behind him.

But on his way out the door, **Theo paused.** He looked back over his shoulder and said in his normal voice, "I really *am* sorry."

Then he was gone. To Jodi, the whole thing seemed a little suspicious.

"I said it before," said Ash. "But he is really getting into his role."

"Maybe," said Jodi. **Or maybe she'd been wrong to give Theo a second chance.**

Chapter 13

THE SHOW MUST GO ON. DON'T LET IT GO ON WITHOUT YOU!

Po wanted to get back to the Minecraft as soon as possible. They all wanted that. But accidentally or not, Theo had done quite a bit of damage to the computers' central power strip. Harper promised to go directly to Doc with the problem. **But even if Doc was able to fix it** immediately, Po feared it would be days before they had time to return to the dungeon.

He was right about that. The next few days were packed with preparation for *The Phantasm of the Cafetorium.*

By the afternoon of the show, **Po had helped out with just about every part of the**

play. He'd finished painting sets with Jodi and making the Phantasm's cardboard gondola with Harper. **(The finished product looked just like a Minecraft boat brought to life!)** He'd also made sure that Morgan was ready for his acting debut.

Ash had started calling Po her "unofficial assistant." It was a title Po embraced with pride. **For one thing, it got him a little closer to the stage.** For another, Po learned a lot by floating from one group to another. In the end, his "role" was to not *have* a role, and that suited him just fine.

In the last minutes before the curtain would go up, Ash gathered the cast and crew backstage. **"I'm amazed at what we've accomplished,"** she told them. "We've built an entire world. And now we're going to dazzle the rest of the school with the story of **the Phantasm.**" She smiled. "I'm about to make my final report to Ms. Minerva. I'll be so happy to tell her we've had no glitches, no unexpected complications—**no problems at all."**

"Uh, Ash?" said Jodi as if on cue. "We've got a big problem."

Ash gripped her clipboard so tightly that her knuckles went white. "What is it?" she asked.

"It's this guy," Jodi answered, pointing at Morgan.

"What, Morgan?" said Po. "No way! He knows his lines, I'm sure of it."

"Oh, he knows his lines," Jodi said, rolling her eyes. **"But he's lost his voice."**

Morgan smiled sheepishly and shrugged as he moved his mouth. Only a faint whisper came out. *"Sorry. . . ."*

"We're doomed!" cried a student on the tech crew.

"It's the curse of the Phantasm!" cried another.

"Nobody panic!" said Ash, and she held out her hands to calm them. "We . . . definitely have a plan B." She cast her eyes all around, clearly trying to form a plan B on the spot.

Her wild eyes landed on Po. "It's Po!" she said. **"Po is our plan B!"**

"Uh, I am?" said Po.

"You know Morgan's dialogue," said Ash.

"But who will run the lights?" Harper asked.

"We're doomed!" said a student.

Po had a flash of inspiration. "Doc can run the lights," he said.

"Doc?" echoed Ash. **"Isn't she banned from backstage?"**

"Yeah, she is," said Po. "But Doc knows how the equipment works, and she can follow directions.

And look . . ." **Po held up his script, marked up with all his notes.** "Directions. They're all written down."

"It seems like a good idea to me," said Jodi.

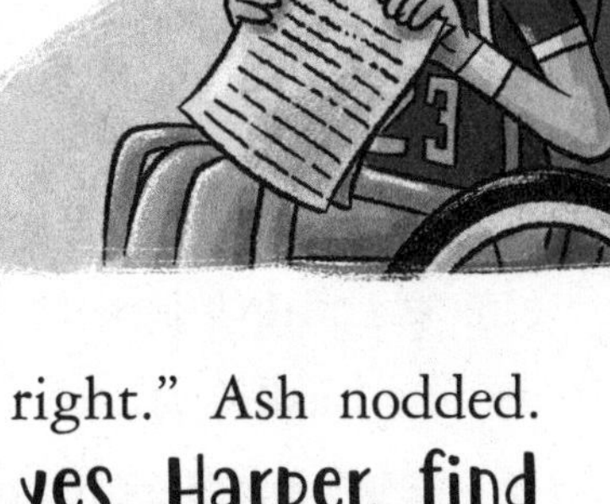

"All right." Ash nodded. **"I say yes. Harper, find Doc and bring her here.** Jodi, let Ms. Minerva know about the change of plan. Morgan, get some soup! And, Po . . . ?"

"Yeah?" said Po.

"Better get into costume," she said. **"Baker Gunther, Monster Hunter, is due on stage in ten minutes!"**

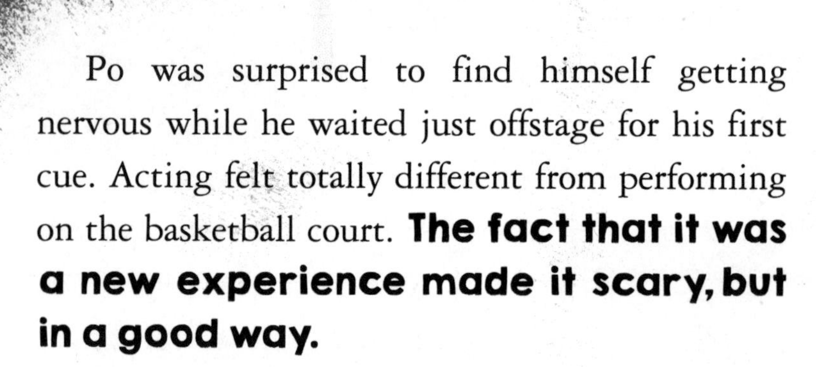

Po was surprised to find himself getting nervous while he waited just offstage for his first cue. Acting felt totally different from performing on the basketball court. **The fact that it was a new experience made it scary, but in a good way.**

Po closed his eyes.

He took three deep breaths.

He told himself he would be fine, no matter what happened out there.

And he wheeled out onstage.

The lights were so bright, he couldn't see the audience at all. But he was pretty sure they were all dressed like chickens. . . .

Theo strode across the stage, wearing his Phantasm costume. **He pulled a cardboard croissant right**

out of Po's hands.

"Ah, there you are!" said Theo. "Just the very thing to satisfy my traitorous hunger!"

Po let himself feel what **Gunther the Baker** would feel in that moment. To have created something precious, only to have it torn from his grasp? Gunther would feel shock and hurt. Disbelief and anger. **Po let the feelings wash over him,** and when he opened his mouth to speak, **he spoke in the anguished voice** of Baker Gunther.

"Unhand that croissant!" he cried.

The delivery was perfect.

And Baker Gunther was just getting started.

Over the next hour, **Po was on and off the stage every few minutes.** His nervousness didn't return even once. When he was backstage, he was Po, spending time with his friends, putting on a play. **When he was in the spotlight, he was Baker Gunther, Monster Hunter.** And Gunther knew no fear. He would bravely pursue the Phantasm into the catacombs beneath the cafetorium. He would get his pastries back if it was the last thing he ever did.

Po thought he would like Gunther if they met in real life.

After he'd spoken his last line of the

night, he returned backstage and pulled the baker's cap from his head. Those lights had been hot, and he was sweating. But he was also smiling a huge smile.

Ash gave him a thumbs-up, even while she was speaking directions into her headset.

Harper gave him a pat on the back.

Jodi said, "**Good job, Po.**"

And Morgan said, "**It was a slam dunk!**"

"Thanks, everybody," Po said. "And could I just say— Waitaminute. Morgan!"

Po's jaw dropped. "**You can talk?**"

"Oops," Morgan said, clapping his hands over his mouth.

Everyone looked shocked. Clearly Morgan had fooled them all.

He was a better actor than anyone had guessed.

"Sorry I was sneaky about it," Morgan said. "But I could tell you wanted to be onstage, Po.

And I wanted everyone to see that you can be an athlete and an actor."

Po felt a rush of gratitude for his friend. "Thanks, Morgan," he said. "I'll admit, I really enjoyed being out there in the spotlight."

They watched the rest of the play from backstage. Po could see the actors onstage, and he also had a view of Doc as she controlled the lights. She looked like she was having the time of her life. Standing at the controls, **she reminded Po of a concert pianist,** totally focused on her task and loving every minute of it.

When it was all over, **Po returned to the center of the stage,** rolling back into the spotlight, and **took a bow.**

The applause thrilled him. And he had an idea. Next year, he could cut back on sports to make time for the drama club. If he planned it, maybe he could find a way to do *both* things.

His coach wouldn't be thrilled with that news. But Po thought he would understand.

It was time for Po to choose his own roles.

Chapter 14

DON'T SAY WE DIDN'T WARN YOU. . . .

Po found Ash as soon as the final curtain had dropped.

"Ash, that was *amazing*," he said. "I can't believe it all came together so well."

Ash gave a wry smile. "Are you saying you doubted me?"

"You? No way," Po answered. "But I thought for sure Baron Sweetcheeks would get loose and cause chaos."

The hamster in Ash's front pocket gave an indignant squeak.

Ms. Minerva swept in and gave them each a hug. "Good job, everyone," she said. "Now,

did either of you happen to notice any Broadway critics or Hollywood scouts in the audience? I think *The Phantasm of the Cafetorium* has a real future!" She peeked out past the curtain at the departing audience. "I sent out invitations but never heard back from anyone. . . ."

As Ms. Minerva slipped past the curtain, **Doc approached Po and Ash.**

"So," she said. "How did I do?"

"Doc, you nailed it!" said Po. "Honestly, you did even better than I could have done."

"I suspect *that's* not true," said Doc. She smiled warmly. "But I appreciate you both finding a way for me to participate. Not only did I enjoy it, **I also got some ideas for automating lights throughout the school.** I really think Minerva will come around when I tell her she can be in a spotlight all day, every day."

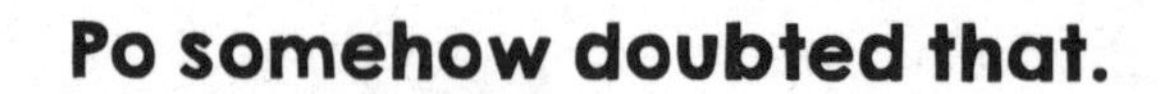

Po somehow doubted that.

"We have a little bit of time before the cast party," Ash said. "Want to get some homework done?"

"I had another idea," said Po. "I asked Doc earlier backstage, and **the computer lab is open again.**"

Ash's eyes lit up. **"Are you suggesting that we fit in a quick game?"**

"I'd say Baker Gunther isn't quite done hunting monsters yet," Po answered. "There's an Evoker King out there who needs to face justice—**flaky, buttery justice!**"

After days of waiting, they were back in Minecraft and again in front of that great vault door.

They looked around for enemies. They checked the door for booby-traps. But all was clear.

They opened the door.

"I don't know what I was expecting," said Po, looking at what stood before them. "But it wasn't that."

There was a single block in the middle of the

room. It floated a few inches above a plinth. **It spun in place like a miniature planet.**

"I THINK IT'S BEDROCK," said Morgan.

"I think you're right," said Ash. "And that's unusual, to say the least."

"Because **BEDROCK** isn't supposed to be loose like that?" Jodi asked.

"NOT IN SURVIVAL MODE," said Harper. "It's not supposed to be collectible, but *that* looks ready to be collected."

"Should we take it?" asked Po.

"NO. I'LL BE TAKING IT," said a voice at their backs.

Po and the others spun quickly around. **There in the open doorway stood a gray-skinned figure with menacing eyes, a blocky nose, and the flowing robes of a spellcaster.** The air around him shimmered with power, and Po knew for certain who this was: the Evoker King, at last.

"YOU CAN TRY TO TAKE IT," said Morgan, and he readied his sword.

The Evoker King didn't flinch. He took a single step forward. "Why stop me now?" he asked. **"AFTER ALL, IT'S YOU WHO CLEARED THE WAY FOR ME."**

"What does *that* mean?" Ash demanded.

"I WAS TELLING THE TRUTH WHEN I WARNED YOU ABOUT THE DANGERS OF THIS DUNGEON," said their foe. "But you assumed my warning was a threat. You assumed this was *my* dungeon, and that the treasure before you was the source of my power. But it's not. It's the heart of this world. And this dungeon was built to keep me away."

"OH NO," said Harper.

"With this **FOUNDATION STONE,** this entire world will be clay in my hands," he said with a sneer. "But I couldn't get by the guards. I knew *you,* however, would figure it out if presented with the right challenge. **SO REALLY, I COULDN'T HAVE DONE THIS WITHOUT YOU."** He smiled an eerie digital smile. **"HERE. LET ME THANK YOU."**

With that, he lifted his arms, and the ripples of power all around him swirled and shimmered. In less time than it took Po to blink, **the Evoker King conjured a swarm of vexes.** The ghostly winged creatures filled the vault, swooping toward them and swinging their swords.

Po stood his ground. He defeated one vex, only to be hit from behind by another.

"I'll get him!" Jodi said, coming to Po's aid. Together, they banished two more vexes in a *poof* of pixels.

Po caught his breath and looked around. **His friends had been victorious.** They were all still standing.

But the floating piece of bedrock was gone. "He took it!" Po cried.

"What would he even want it for?" asked Harper.

"What does it *do*?" asked Ash.

"AND IF HE DIDN'T BUILD THIS DUNGEON, WHO DID?" Jodi wondered.

"I don't know the answers to any of those questions," Morgan said. His square shoulders slumped. "I only know that he beat us. **THE EVOKER KING WON!"**

"He won this round," said Po. "But he's all alone in here. And we have each other." He looked at his friends. Their cube faces wore frowns and their brows were furrowed. "**HE'S TRYING TO CONVINCE US THAT WE'RE LOSERS. BUT THAT'S A ROLE I DON'T ACCEPT.** And neither should any of you!"

"What can we do?" Morgan asked. "He's been a step ahead of us all along."

"Then we stop chasing him," said Po. "We've got to come at this from a different angle. And I think . . . **THEO MIGHT BE THE KEY.**"

"Theo?" said Harper. "Are you sure he can be trusted?"

"I'm not sure," Po answered. **"BUT I LEARNED RECENTLY THAT HE KNOWS HOW TO CODE. AND THAT COULD GIVE US A HUGE ADVANTAGE HERE."**

He saw his friends exchange a look. "It's an interesting idea," Ash said at last.

"You're right, Po," Morgan said. "We've been running from the Evoker King for too long."

"It's time to reverse the roles," Po said. "We're going after him!"

MINECRAFT is a game about placing blocks and going on adventures. Build, play, and explore across infinitely generated worlds of mountains, caverns, oceans, jungles, and deserts. Defeat hordes of zombies, bake the cake of your dreams, venture to new dimensions, or build a skyscraper. What you do in Minecraft is up to you.

Nick Eliopulos is a writer who lives in Brooklyn (as many writers do). He likes to spend half his free time reading and the other half gaming. He cowrote the Adventurers Guild series with his best friend and works as a narrative designer for a small video game studio. After all these years, Endermen still give him the creeps.

Luke Flowers is an author-illustrator living in Colorado Springs with his wife and three children. He is grateful to have had the opportunity to illustrate forty-five books since 2014, when he began living his lifelong dream of illustrating children's books. Luke has also written and illustrated a best-selling book series called Moby Shinobi. When he's not illustrating in his creative cave, he enjoys performing puppetry, playing basketball, and going on adventures with his family.

Chris Hill is an illustrator living in Birmingham, England, with his wife and two daughters and has been loving it for twenty-five years! When he's not working, he loves spending time with his family and trying to tire out his dog on long walks. If there's any time left after that, he loves to go riding on his motorcycle, feeling the wind on his face while contemplating his next illustration adventure.

JOURNEY INTO THE WORLD OF MINECRAFT™

—BOOKS FOR EVERY READING LEVEL—

Read all of the Woodsword Chronicles!

Discover more Minecraft adventures:

Learn about the latest Minecraft books when you sign up for our newsletter at **ReadMinecraft.com**

Penguin Random House

MOJANG